This book belongs to

Written by Elanor Best.
Illustrated by Lara Ede.

Taylor Tiptoe

Elanor Best • Lara Ede

make
believe
ideas

Tiny **Taylor** loved to *dance*:
her **feet** would NEVER stop.

She'd **spin** and twist

and

Leap and *twirl*,

then

shimmy,

shake and **hop**.

For this year's Summer Showcase, **Taylor** longed to get the *chance* to play the leading **princess** part and **prove** that she could *dance*.

But every time poor **Taylor** tried
to strike a perfect *pose*,
no one seemed to notice
in the sea of *pointed toes.*

In fact, she was so **LITTLE**

and so **VERY** hard to spot,

the other dancers *passed* right by

this tiny *tutu* dot!

"There's just **one** *dancer* who can help:

the magic Queen Delphine."

So, on her tiptoes **Taylor** skipped along the *winding* street...

and **didn't** stop until she stood
at Delphine's pointed feet.

"My only wish is to be tall," said Taylor, feeling brave.

"I can **help**," the **queen** replied,
and gave her **wand** a *wave*.

Sparkles
fizzled in the air,
around small **Taylor's** toes.

And then she *gasped*
as she began....

...to grow

and grow

and
grow!

Now **Taylor** was

GINORMOUS!

She **towered** above the floor,
and **gazed** around at all the things
she **hadn't** seen before.

Queen Delphine's
Dancing School

But back at school, when **Taylor** danced, *everything* went wrong.

She couldn't keep her *balance*
for her **legs** were far too long.

Worst of all, now she was *tall,*
she found she had to duck.
She **couldn't** get through **any** door
without first getting **stuck!**

Taylor rushed back to the queen
to see what she could do.

"I've got a plan," wise Delphine said. "Now try just being YOU!"

"The secret to good *dancing* is **not** your **looks** or **height**. It's something *within* YOU that **shines** much **brighter** than the lights!"

Now **Taylor** knew just what to do
to get on with her mission.

She **puffed** her chest
and took a **breath**....

then ran to the audition.

With **bravery,** she *leapt* on stage and **pointed** both her feet.

She *whirled* and whizzed and bounced and *fizzed*

and **boogied** to the **beat.**

The *music* stopped, and all at once
the *judges* gave a cheer.

They shouted, **Tiny Taylor**
is the *princess* for this year!"

Summer SHOWCASE

starring
(the tiny but terrific...)

Taylor Tiptoe

For one night only

Queen Delphine's Dancing School Auditorium

Tickets on the door

At last, the Summer Showcase came, and **Taylor** played her part.

She *danced* the best, despite her size,
for she danced with all her **heart!**

Taylor's wish had made her learn the **one** thing that was **true:** there's nothing that you **can't** achieve if you *believe* in **YOU!**

Royal box